iDRAKULA

iDRAKULA

BEKKA BLACK

sourcebooks
fire

Published by Sourcebooks Fire, an imprint of Sourcebooks, Inc.
P.O. Box 4410, Naperville, Illinois 60567-4410
(630) 961-3900
Fax: (630) 961-2168
teenfire.sourcebooks.com

Library of Congress Cataloging-in-Publication data is on file with the publisher.

Printed and bound in the United States of America.
VP 10 9 8 7 6 5 4 3 2 1

To my son, my husband,
and my cell phone

June 11 8:14 PM

Renfield had a psychotic break. Carted off to Bellevue. More l8r

Wth? Details?

June 11 8:16 PM

Jonathan?

From: Jonathan Harker
To: Mina Murray
Subject: Renfield
Sent: June 11 9:02 PM

Mina,

Here's Mr. Renfield's take on it:

>Harker,
>As I am sure you are aware, my son Randolph is indisposed.
>He was scheduled to fly to Bucharest tomorrow to meet
>with an important client. Can you go in his stead? The
>client requested you specifically, as Randolph apparently
>discussed you with him. The client was quite insistent.
>Although you are only a summer intern, I trust that we can
>quickly train you to carry out Randolph's duties
>satisfactorily. As I'm sure you are aware, it is a wonderful
>opportunity for you. Please make your own flight
>arrangements and then fill out an expense report for
>reimbursement.

Then he rattled on like always. Indisposed? They hauled
Renfield Jr. past me screaming. He actually bit the head off a
little gray mouse he caught in the cafeteria.

Short version: I'm off to Romania tomorrow. First time out
of the country by myself. Wow, huh? How could I say no to a
free trip to Europe?

I'll be stuck here in the cubicle catacombs until the middle of
the night getting ready.

Want to swing by my dad's tomorrow and ride with me to the airport?

I know Renfield Jr. and Lucy haven't seen each other in months, but somebody should tell her what happened to him. I'm sure Renfield Sr. won't.

Sorry I'll miss your jujitsu tournament. You'll just have to kick butt alone.

J

From: Tepes Travel
To: Jonathan Harker
Subject: Your Trip to Bucharest
Sent: June 11 9:02 PM

****

THANK YOU! Travel Reservation Confirmation
****

Dear Jonathan:
Thank you for booking your travel through Tepes Travel.

Your trip to Otopeni Bucharest Airport (OTP), approximately 12.4 miles from Bucharest city central, is confirmed. A summary of your reservation is provided below.

Your Tepes Travel Trip ID is 3141 5926 5358

Ticket(s) issued on Thu, Jun 11 at 09:01 PM EST.

****

ITINERARY
****

For your boarding pass, use reference code QENDYN for online or airport check-in.

Fri, June 12
New York, NY (JFK) to Otopeni Bucharest (OTP)

Flight: Delta Airlines KL 9080 operated by KLM Royal Dutch Airlines

Depart: 3:55 p.m., New York, NY (JFK)
Arrive: 6:00 a.m., Amsterdam Sat June 13 (one day later)

Flight: KLM 2701, operated by KLM Royal Dutch Airlines
Depart: 2:15 p.m., Amsterdam
Arrive: 6:10 p.m. Otopeni Bucharest (OTP)

Total Travel Time: 19 hrs 15 mins

****

PRICING

****

1 adult: $949.20
Taxes & fees: $110.00
Total: $1059.20

June 12 1:30 AM

Where r u?

Getting Lucy home. She puked. Ewww

Wear gloves. Lol. C u tomorrow?

Of course. How's Renfield?

Nothing new

Can't believe u r deserting me for the wilds of Romania tomorrow!!! Will miss u

Wide Web World of Maps

◄ ► ⊡ ✚ | http://www.widewebworldofmaps.romania.vi |

ROMANIA

- CUJU - NAPOCA
- IASI
- TIMISOARA
- BRASOV
- BUCURESTI
- CONSTANTA

MAP OF ROMANIA
Click PLAY to view interactive map & audio guide ▶

VIEW O
OTHER
AFRICA
ANTART
ASIA
AUSTRA
EUROPE
• Rom
- Ro
Get

NORTH
SOUTH

Sights to see in Romania:

- Castles
- Medieval Cities
- Wooden Churches
- Painted Monastaries
- **Romantic Getaways**
- Black Sea Resorts
- Spas

Win a trip to Romania!
Click here to see how

iD

My Favorite Romantic Destination is
♥ ♥ ♥ Constanta, Romania ♥ ♥ ♥

I love Constanta!

I love Constanta because my boyfriend proposed to me here. We took a trip to the coast and spent the day studying the Roman mosaics and walking on the beach.

At sunset we climbed up the Genoese lighthouse. It is not so high a climb.

We held hands and looked out over the waters that Jason and the Argonauts crossed with the Golden Fleece. When the last red traces of the sun fell below the horizon, Alexandru dropped down onto one knee. At first I thought he was hurt. But then he pulled out a ring, and I knew.

He asked me to marry him.

I stared at him for a few seconds until he asked, "Well?" in a voice like a little boy.

And I said, "Yes, yes, and yes!"

We walked along by the casino after that, and I don't think my feet touched the ground even one time.

iD

June 13 2:03 PM

Landed safe no sleep on plane

Poor baby

Rain is pissing down here. Hope I can find count's driver

Maybe next time we can go together. Might be romantic...

U think everywhere is romantic. So far, ur wrong about romania

I luv u

behave

hard for me

keep it soft

Lol

bye

La revedere!

in a strait jacket

Gotta board count's SUV. Driver too creepy

Treat him to the gun show

Ha ha he's big enough to eat me

I'll arm wrestle him for u

How was the tournament?

The 16-17 age bracket is hard! I only came in second

Congrats!!!

Recipe Central | Online Recipe Source

http://recipecentralonline.myrecipebook.chick

Welcome!   Log In | Join!

Recipe Central

Recipes ▾   Ingredients ▾   More ▾

Similar Recipes   My Recipe Book

| Print | Share | Save | paprika hendl | Search |

Paprika Hendl ★★★☆☆
Signature dish of Romania. Spicy.

Serves 4

Ingredients:
3 cups chicken broth
1 ½ pounds chicken, cooked
  and cut into strips
¼ cup butter or margarine
1 onion, diced
3 heaping teaspoons paprika
1 clove garlic

2 tablespoons flour
1 cup sour cream or yogurt
4 cups spätzle noodles,
  cooked

Directions:
Saute onion, garlic, and chicken in butter.
Add the sautéed mixture to broth and paprika in a pan.
  Slowly add flour to thicken. Simmer for 30 minutes. Add
  half of the sour cream.
Serve over spätzle with a dollop of sour cream on top.
Fetească Neagră (black maiden) wine is a good complement to
  the dish.

iD

Bathory Catering | Packages | Romanian Evening

http://www.bathorycatering.cm/packages_rom

Bathory Catering

Romanian Evening

Home
Services
Packages
Pricing
Specials
Contact

Enjoy the culinary delights of Bucharest from the comforts of your own home! Food comes ready to serve. Servers wear traditional Romanian folk costumes.

Menu includes:

— *Ciorbă de fasole cu afumătură* (sour bean and smoked meat soup)

— Delicious chicken paprikash with spätzle noodles and sour cream

— *Clatites* (chocolate-filled crepes)

$23.00 per person, minimum 8 orders.
Drinks extra.

iD

From: Mina Murray
To: Jonathan Harker
Subject: Renfield slipping in and out
Sent: June 13 8:27 PM

Jonathan,

I miss you. I wish you could have come when we visited Renfield today. Am attaching a photo of the gates. Kinda cool looking, but only if you know you can get right back out.

He looks terrible. He's lost about 20 pounds and his face is yellowish. It was the saddest thing I've ever seen. I didn't cry, but my eyes got full and I had to do that blinky thing you hate.

Lucy stared at him with her mouth open, like a bird at a snake, so I had to do the talking. Why do I always have to step in and do the yucky stuff? Here's how it went:

Renfield: I must consume life forces to be strong. He decreed it. He has come to me even here. And He decreed it.

Me (keeping one eye on the door and wishing you were there): Randy, how are you?

Renfield: Weak. I must eat live meat. Could you get me a kitten? A soft little kitten?

Me: No. (Eww. Do you think he'd really eat one?)

Renfield: How about a bird? Or a spider? Or even a fly? Carnivores are better because they've already consumed life forces. You understand?

Me: No. (And I don't want to either. Not ever.)

Then he started to cry and said it was the only way. He wrapped his arms around his knees and rocked and cried. Lucy stood frozen, so I had to hug him and tell him everything would be ok. And he smelled bad. But it had to be done. I couldn't leave him there crying all alone.

After that, Lucy actually hit on this premed student who is interning there. Right in front of Renfield. And he wasn't so out of it that he didn't notice. The premed guy seemed ok. Gorgeous and blond, as that's Lucy's new type. Abraham Van Helsing. Dutch. Poor guy's totally helpless under Lucy's spell, like most guys (except you). Still, I wish she'd stop dating totally random guys. Worries me.

Hope you arrived at the Count's and got a good night's sleep finally, poor baby!

Love,
Mina

- - - - - - - - - - - - - - -Attachment Below- - - - - - - - - - - - - - -

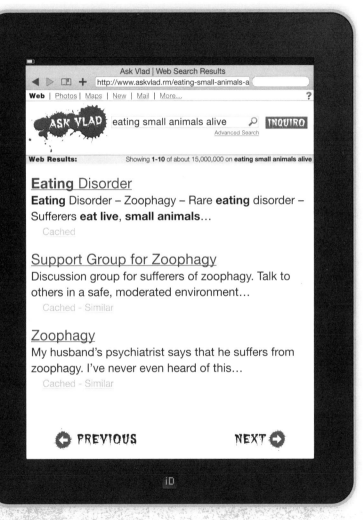

From: Jonathan Harker
To: Mina Murray
Subject: Re: Renfield slipping in and out
Sent: June 13 9:09 PM

Mina,

I hope you get this. The Count's daughter gave me a local mail server to use because the government won't let me access the firm's. Something about stopping spammers here from hacking mail servers back in the States.

I want to come home. Now. Seriously. Well, almost.

The Count lives in an old stone castle. One side opens onto a cliff. You can practically see the barbarians smashing up against it. The whole place is surrounded by bats at night. Wish I'd brought a taser. I'm attaching a picture here I took on the drive up. The Count "bid me welcome" with a bow and in perfect archaic English. He says things like "good sir." It's like he's a 100 years old. Guess that's just a good European education.

But he's creepy. He's pale as a bone and looks older than anyone I've ever seen. His skin is all weird. It's thin and wrinkly, like tracing paper that was rolled into a ball and then smoothed out. He also smells bad.

Luckily, I won't be here long. Renfield did all the real work with him last time he was here. The Count didn't ask much about Renfield, even though they've been working together for months. And I wasn't supposed to bring it up. But he did have a picture of Renfield and Lucy and you and me lying on his desk. He said Renfield printed it off of his phone. It was the one where we were all dressed up in Renaissance costume, right before my senior prom. Remember that? Your dress was lower cut in the photo than I remember, BTW.

He's shipping three giant ebony boxes of dirt to Manhattan. They look like double coffins. When I asked why, he said he has something he wants to grow there that will not "flourish in foreign soil." He doesn't want the dirt to be sterilized, although I don't know how it'll get past customs. Apparently Renfield convinced him to ship it in a container with his household goods because they almost never check them.

Have to get back to dinner. The Count is hosting a farewell party, and the legal drinking age in Romania is 18. I am finally old enough to drink legally somewhere!

J

- - - - - - - - - - - - - - -Attachment Below- - - - - - - - - - - - - - -

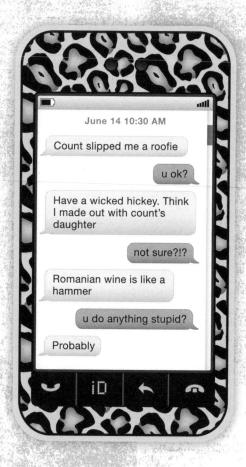

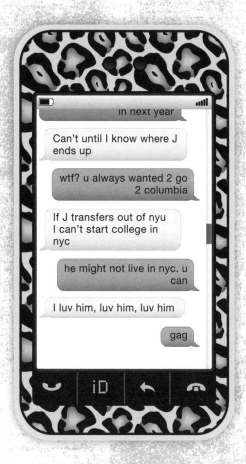

in next year

Can't until I know where J ends up

wtf? u always wanted 2 go 2 columbia

If J transfers out of nyu I can't start college in nyc

he might not live in nyc. u can

I luv him, luv him, luv him

gag

From: Jonathan Harker
To: Mina Murray
Subject: Phone dead
Sent: June 14 11:13 AM

Mina,

Could barely drag myself out of bed this morning. Big flask of Romanian wine = big hangover. Coincidence?

I am going to go look for the Count and see if he has any aspirin. Hope I can keep it down. My head is throbbing, I'm queasy, and the bright sunlight hurts my eyes. All self-inflicted, I know. Doesn't make me feel any better.

Cell battery is dead and my adapter is broken. Only a matter of time before the laptop goes, too, I guess. Glad I'm leaving soon. Will call from the Bucharest airport with my flight details. Meet me by the baggage claim?

J

From: Jonathan Harker
To: Mina Murray
Subject: Locked in
Sent: June 14 3:32 PM

Mina,

I ransacked the house, except a few locked rooms. It's eerie. It feels like no one really lives here. I know the place should be empty because he's packed everything, but there are drifts of dust and tattered cobwebs everywhere. It's like no one has set foot in this house in years. The only clean rooms are mine and the dining hall.

These giant wooden shutters are closed everywhere, too. Guess that keeps out the bats that have banged against my window all night. I am exhausted, and yes, it's more than the hangover.

I can't find the Count. He must have accidentally locked me in this pile of rock. Crap.

Can't even find his servants or his daughter.

I don't like this place. I want out.

It's cold, and it smells bad, like something died in the walls. Except the walls are solid stone.

Miss u. Why aren't you emailing me back?

J

From: Mina Murray
To: Jonathan Harker
Subject: You ok?
Sent: June 14 5:05 PM

Jonathan,

I am worried about you. Haven't heard anything since you told me about the Count smuggling dirt to the U.S. Are you sure that's a good idea? Is that even legal? Who knows what microbes might be in that soil?

Hope you didn't drink too much at that farewell dinner and do something stupid (like usual).

I went to the cemetery with Lucy today. It's been exactly nine months since her mom died. At least she didn't cry this time. I did. I kept thinking of you dying. Morbid, I know, but I got chills inside that crypt. Someday we're all going to end up in a box. Alone.

Lucy has fallen for the premed guy! He was all she talked about. He sounds normal and stable, like the kind of guy she doesn't usually give a second glance. I'm the one who likes nice guys, so it's weird to see Lucy interested in one. Still, I have to admit he's awfully hot. (I threw that in to see if you are paying attention. Were you?)

Me, I'd like to know what's up with Renfield. He's always been a bit creepy, but it's awful to think of him locked away like an animal. It's a different box from Lucy's mom's, but it feels as permanent and as lonely. And he's still alive. Got the chills again.

They say he's in isolation for his own protection. I don't know about that, but I'm sure scared of the thought of him stalking around eating kittens. What do you suppose set him off? Was he ok when he got back from Romania last time? Maybe it's something in the water... :)

Seriously, be careful. I want you back safe.

Miss u. C u soon, I hope.

Off to work out at the dojo! Will tell Sensei John you said salut.

Love,
Mina

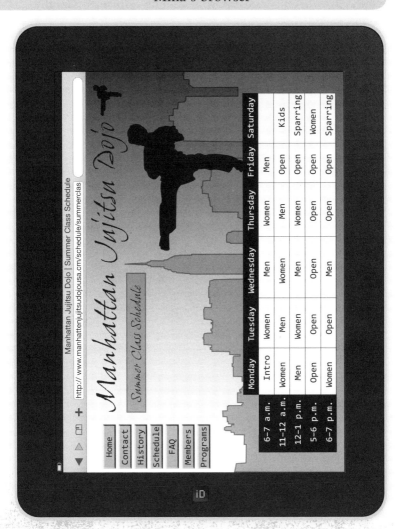

From: Jonathan Harker
To: Mina Murray
Subject: Count back
Sent: June 14 8:47 PM

Mina,

Count came back right after sunset. He's all weird and creepy, hissing like a lizard.

It gets so dark here. Not like in the city. The dark is so thick it practically climbs down my throat and smothers me. I can't see my hand in front of my face. Have to use a candle to get into bed. A candle. Like in a horror movie.

Tomorrow the SUV will schlep me through the bats to the airport. I hope.

Wish you were here. I can think of a few things we could do in the dark without parents around...Why aren't you emailing me back?

J

From: Jonathan Harker
To: Mina Murray
Subject: Locked in again
Sent: June 15 6:06 AM

Mina,

Count gone. Locked in house. I know it sounds paranoid, but I think it's not an accident. I've tried every door and window. Only way out is to jump 100 feet into that rushing river. After another day alone here, I might chance it.

Am getting more and more exhausted. Can't sleep because of the freakin' bats. Have bad dreams if I do manage to doze off. Blood and death. I know, you'll say it's the paprika. But I'm not so sure.

Count never eats. He's been here for dinner every night but never eats. Or drinks. When I asked him about that while he was filling my goblet, he said, "I never drink...wine." I've never seen him drink anything.

What if he's poisoning me?

Call Renfield's dad and tell him to get me the hell out of here.

Miss u.

J

From:	Jonathan Harker
To:	Lucy Westenra
Subject:	Freaking out
Sent:	June 15 6:16 AM

Lucy,

My phone is dead. Can't charge the laptop either. I'm starting to freak out here.

I'm trapped in the castle. I think the Count locked me in. When I got back to my room, I noticed that there was blood on my pillow. I think it's from that hickey. There are puncture wounds in the middle of it. Oh crap. What happened to me last night?

Don't tell Mina. She'll panic. But call my dad and tell him to get a hold of Mr. Renfield and get me the hell out of here. I'd call him myself, but the Count doesn't have a phone in the whole castle.

I am not screwing around here, Lucy. Please help me out.

J

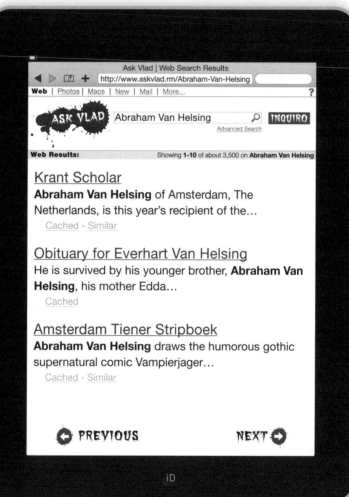

Ask Vlad | Web Search Results

http://www.askvlad.rm/Abraham-Van-Helsing

Web | Photos | Maps | New | Mail | More...   ?

ASK VLAD   Abraham Van Helsing   🔍 **INQUIRO**
                                    Advanced Search

Web Results: Showing **1-10** of about 3,500 on **Abraham Van Helsing**

Krant Scholar
Abraham Van Helsing of Amsterdam, The
Netherlands, is this year's recipient of the...
   Cached - Similar

Obituary for Everhart Van Helsing
He is survived by his younger brother, **Abraham Van
Helsing**, his mother Edda...
   Cached

Amsterdam Tiener Stripboek
Abraham Van Helsing draws the humorous gothic
supernatural comic Vampierjager...
   Cached - Similar

⬅ PREVIOUS   **NEXT ➡**

iD

From: Postmaster
To: Jonathan Harker
Subject: Undelivered mail
Sent: June 15 7:40 PM

This is an automatically generated Delivery Status Notification.

THIS IS A WARNING MESSAGE ONLY.
YOU DO NOT NEED TO RESEND YOUR MESSAGE.

Delivery to the following recipients has been delayed due to server problems.

Mina Murray

--Forwarded Message Attachment--
From: Jonathan Harker
To: Mina Murray
Subject: Phone dead

From:	Postmaster
To:	Jonathan Harker
Subject:	Undelivered mail
Sent:	June 15 7:40 PM

This is an automatically generated Delivery Status Notification.

THIS IS A WARNING MESSAGE ONLY.
YOU DO NOT NEED TO RESEND YOUR MESSAGE.

Delivery to the following recipients has been delayed due to server problems.

Mina Murray

--Forwarded Message Attachment--
From: Jonathan Harker
To: Mina Murray
Subject: Locked in

From: Postmaster
To: Jonathan Harker
Subject: Undelivered mail
Sent: June 15 7:40 PM

This is an automatically generated Delivery Status Notification.

THIS IS A WARNING MESSAGE ONLY.
YOU DO NOT NEED TO RESEND YOUR MESSAGE.

Delivery to the following recipients has been delayed due to server problems.

Mina Murray

--Forwarded Message Attachment--
From: Jonathan Harker
To: Mina Murray
Subject: Count back

From:	Postmaster
To:	Jonathan Harker
Subject:	Undelivered mail
Sent:	June 15 7:40 PM

This is an automatically generated Delivery Status Notification.

THIS IS A WARNING MESSAGE ONLY.
YOU DO NOT NEED TO RESEND YOUR MESSAGE.

Delivery to the following recipients has been delayed due to server problems.

Mina Murray

--Forwarded Message Attachment--
From: Jonathan Harker
To: Mina Murray
Subject: Locked in again

From:	Postmaster
To:	Jonathan Harker
Subject:	Undelivered mail
Sent:	June 15 7:40 PM

This is an automatically generated Delivery Status Notification.

THIS IS A WARNING MESSAGE ONLY.
YOU DO NOT NEED TO RESEND YOUR MESSAGE.

Delivery to the following recipients has been delayed due to server problems.

Lucy Westenra

--Forwarded Message Attachment--
From: Jonathan Harker
To: Lucy Westenra
Subject: Freaking out

From:	Jonathan Harker
To:	Mina Murray
Subject:	I love you
Sent:	June 15 7:42 PM

My dearest Mina,

All my emails bounced. No news in or out. Cell battery long gone. Laptop battery blinking red. All day no Count.

I broke into one of the locked rooms. It has piles of bones. Human bones. Tiny skulls, like from children. I know that sounds crazy. This whole thing is crazy. I have to get out of here before they kill me, too.

Am jumping out the window with phone and laptop in plastic bags, just in case that's all they find.

Have to get the police here. Or Interpol. Or whatever they have. The Count must be stopped. Even in Romania you can't just kill people.

If this somehow gets through, know that I love you. I've done some stuff I regret, but you aren't one of them.

Cross your fingers for me.

Love,
J

From: Postmaster
To: Jonathan Harker
Subject: Undelivered mail
Sent: June 15 8:06 PM

This is an automatically generated Delivery Status Notification.

THIS IS A WARNING MESSAGE ONLY.
YOU DO NOT NEED TO RESEND YOUR MESSAGE.

Delivery to the following recipients has been delayed.

Mina Murray

--Forwarded Message Attachment--
From: Jonathan Harker
To: Mina Murray
Subject: I love you

From: Mina Murray
To: Frank Renfield
Subject: Jonathan's contact info?
Sent: June 16 9:05 AM

Hello Mr. Renfield,

I'm sorry to bother you, but I haven't heard from Jonathan for three days, which is very out of character. Has he phoned into the office? Is he all right?

I visited Randy about three days ago. He seemed disoriented. He also complained that he doesn't see anyone and is very lonely. I will visit him again today. I'm sure he'll get through it all ok.

Mina Murray

From: Frank Renfield
To: Mina Murray
Subject: Re: Jonathan's contact info?
Sent: June 16 9:15 AM

Mina,

An agent for the Count contacted me and said that Jonathan would be there for a few more days wrapping things up. There are complications with a few of the items to be shipped. The agent mentioned that Jonathan was having problems with his electronic toys, by which I assume he meant the phone and laptop. He lives in a very rural part of Romania, so, unlike New York, they do not have cell phone towers and Internet service providers on every corner. I am certain Jonathan himself will get in touch with both you and me as soon as he is able.

I appreciate your visits to Randolph. Once the doctors ascertain what went wrong, they hope to be able to cure him. Many of his friends have abandoned him, and I am grateful that you have not.

Frank Renfield

From:	Mina Murray
To:	Jonathan Harker
Subject:	Call me
Sent:	June 16 8:10 PM

Jonathan,

I am getting super frantic. It's not like you to stay out of touch. Lucy says it's probably a battery issue and said you probably forgot your adapter. Mr. Renfield says so, too, but it feels wrong. Still, I am going to pretend that they're right.

We saw Renfield again. Here's exactly what he said:

Renfield: The Master is coming.

Me (massively creeped out): What master?

Renfield: Jonathan Harker will be sorry that he stole him. He will.

Me (wondering about the whole last names thing): Stole who?

Renfield: A kitten, Mina Murray. Get me just a little soft kitten. Only one. I only need one.

He started screaming and came at me. I hated to do it, but I used a wrist lock on him. It worked, just like in a tournament. Unlike a tournament, I almost panicked. Almost.

Abe (that premed student Lucy's gaga over) was in the room with us. I held Renfield down until the doctor sedated him, which took a bit because Abe had to run out to get help. He wanted to take over from me and have me go, but Renfield kept trying to move and I was afraid I was going to have to break his wrist or he was going to come at me again. There was no way I was going to let go of him at that point.

Lucy was no help at all. She smashed herself flat against the wall and wouldn't come near us, like crazy is contagious. I'd be mad at her, but she was so upset I didn't have the heart.

It took two shots of whatever it was. After I got out, I had to go throw up.

Renfield has chewed his fingernails to nubs. He makes my skin crawl, but I also feel really sorry for him. (Except when he's attacking me.)

You should visit him when you get home. If he's properly restrained.

It can't help Renfield any to see Lucy so happy. Maybe this guy is THE ONE that she's always looking for. He's old, twenty or so. But it's the happiest I've seen her since her mom died. Wonder what her dad will say? A doctor-to-be is better than her usual losers.

Call me. I'm trying not to be worried, but I'm failing.

I want to know you're ok.

Love,
Mina

June 16 8:35 PM

what u up 2?

Driving myself crazy
worrying about J

stop. come out with me
instead

Where?

ny blood center charity ball
to raise $$ and awareness of
need for blood donors

I don't have a gown

I don't have a gown

i'll loan u one cinderella. u know u can't resist a good cause

June 16 8:37 PM

Maybe

u could even give blood. and there's a chocolate fountain...way better than sitting home alone

Ok

and u might meet a nice rich guy

guy

I'm with J, remember?

not married

Whatever

ur funeral. some of those rich guys will be hot

From: Mina Murray
To: Jonathan Harker
Subject: Call me
Sent: June 17 10:39 AM

Jonathan,

Call me. Your voice mail is full. Why aren't you answering your email?

I went out with Lucy last night. Here's a picture. We went to a charity ball full of lacrosse players who made jokes about their sticks. You see how low I have sunk without you. Come home before things get worse. :)

How can Lucy stand those guys? Abe is way better than them, smart and funny and sensitive. I hope she sticks with him.

Worried about you,
Mina

- - - - - - - - - - - - - - - -Attachment Below- - - - - - - - - - - - - - -

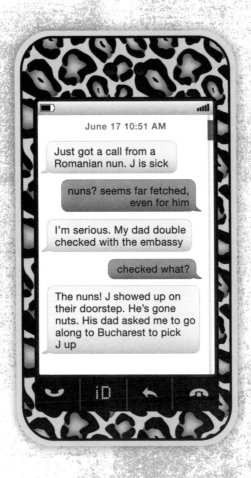

June 17 10:51 AM

Just got a call from a Romanian nun. J is sick

nuns? seems far fetched, even for him

I'm serious. My dad double checked with the embassy

checked what?

The nuns! J showed up on their doorstep. He's gone nuts. His dad asked me to go along to Bucharest to pick J up

along to Bucharest to pick
J up

r u going?

Of course

i'll b right over

From:	Abraham Van Helsing
To:	Mina Murray
Subject:	Delicate question
Sent:	June 17 11:02 AM

Hello Mina,

I know that this is very irregular, and I apologize for this email out of the sky. I am concerned about Lucy. Yesterday she visited with Renfield again. His doctor thought that her presence might help him, as I am sure that you know that they were once intimate friends.

Unfortunately, it went awry. Lucy and Renfield ran into each other's arms like lovers, then sat tailor-style on the floor of his room grunting at one another. I know that's hard to believe, but it is so.

When I made a move to remove her, they started using words. Renfield said that it was his fault, then again that it was his joy.

Renfield said that he had been chosen, and Lucy had been chosen because of him. That she would take her place at the master's side now. I warned Lucy not to buy into his psychosis, but she seemed to regardless.

Then, Renfield leaned forward and said, "We will move beyond death."

I tried to jump between them, but I was too slow.

He and Lucy embraced. He bit her and she bit him back. They drew blood from each other's necks. I called for help and got him off her as soon as I could. He's under the highest security now. They gave both of them a tetanus shot and cleaned the wounds. Lucy laughed it off and called me a prude, but I find it most peculiar. Perhaps this is just some kind of New York ritual that we would never do in Holland?

Her father says she is sleeping now and seems very lethargic overall.

I know you are her friend. Are she and Renfield still involved in an intimate relationship? Is this biting normal for them? I do not wish to ask you to break confidences, but if this is not normal for them, then I am at a loss.

Apologies again for the odd contact. I care deeply about Lucy, and I am worried.

Abe

From: Mina Murray
To: Abraham Van Helsing
Subject: Re: Delicate question
Sent: June 17 11:05 AM

Abe,

Only have a minute. My boyfriend, Jonathan, is very ill.

I thought that Lucy and Renfield had been over for months. She dumped him after her mother died because he was into the occult and resurrection, and all of that suddenly wasn't very funny to her anymore, as you can imagine.

You should ask her yourself. She's a free spirit and does all kinds of wild things, so nothing would surprise me. I know it seems strange, but if Lucy says it's normal for her, it probably is.

Mina

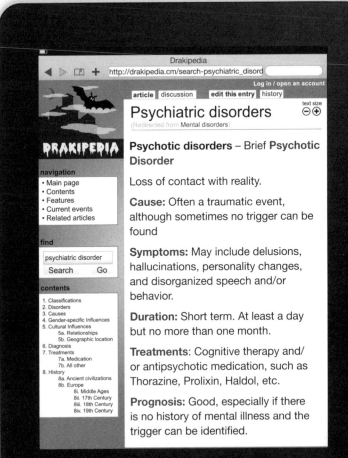

Drakipedia

http://drakipedia.cm/search-psychiatric_disord

Log in / open an account

article | discussion | edit this entry | history

Psychiatric disorders

(Redirected from Mental disorders)

text size ⊖ ⊕

DRAKIPEDIA

navigation
· Main page
· Contents
· Features
· Current events
· Related articles

find

psychiatric disorder

Search | Go

contents
1. Classifications
2. Disorders
3. Causes
4. Gender-specific Influences
5. Cultural Influences
    5a. Relationships
    5b. Geographic location
6. Diagnosis
7. Treatments
    7a. Medication
    7b. All other
8. History
    8a. Ancient civilizations
    8b. Europe
        8i. Middle Ages
        8ii. 17th Century
        8iii. 18th Century
        8iv. 19th Century

Psychotic disorders – Brief **Psychotic Disorder**

Loss of contact with reality.

Cause: Often a traumatic event, although sometimes no trigger can be found

Symptoms: May include delusions, hallucinations, personality changes, and disorganized speech and/or behavior.

Duration: Short term. At least a day but no more than one month.

Treatments: Cognitive therapy and/or antipsychotic medication, such as Thorazine, Prolixin, Haldol, etc.

Prognosis: Good, especially if there is no history of mental illness and the trigger can be identified.

iD

From: Mina Murray
To: Jonathan Harker
Subject: The cavalry is coming
Sent: June 17 11:10 AM

Jonathan,

I don't know if you have Internet access where you are but am sending this just in case. Your father and I are coming to get you and bring you home. I'm sending this from JFK airport (see the picture?), so know that we are only hours away (13 or so, I think). Even though this is so not the romantic trip to Romania that I imagined for us. :)

My mom had a fit when I asked if I could go to Romania to pick you up, even accompanied by your dad. You would have thought I'd asked to join a Transylvanian death cult to hear her carry on.

I only got sketchy news from the embassy. They said that you are sick and upset. I can't tell if it's worse than I think or better.

So, I've decided to go with better.

I miss you, but I'll see you very, very soon. Then we'll bust you out of that nunnery (isn't that supposed to be your job, busting ME out of nunneries?) and get you home.

Love,
Mina

- - - - - - - - - - - - - -Attachment Below- - - - - - - - - - - - - - -

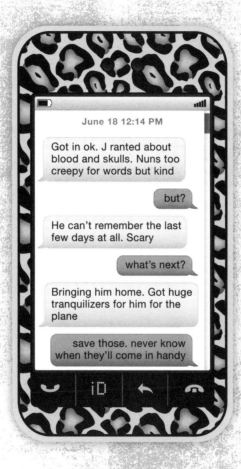

save these. never know
when they'll come in handy

Not funny

how u holding up?

Scared for J. He's like a little
child

good thing u spent all that
time baby-sitting

Again not funny

sorry. not feeling well
myself

Serious?

Serious?

probably just lack of sleep. wacky dutchman

Weird question?

finally, something good. go ahead

Did Renfield bite u?

loose lipped dutchman. yes. no big deal

Big deal. That's really gross. And unsanitary

like sex?

like sex?

What if he had some disease? Or what if he kept biting and u bled to death?

i thought it might help him. abe wouldn't have let it get out of hand

Help him how?

we did something like that once before. i thought it might bring him back

How?

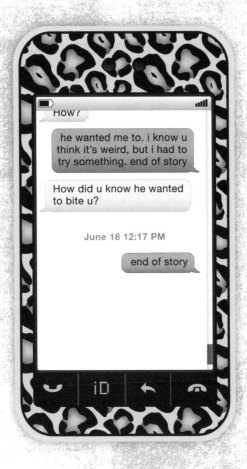

How?

he wanted me to. i know u think it's weird, but i had to try something. end of story

How did u know he wanted to bite u?

June 18 12:17 PM

end of story

From: Mina Murray
To: Lucy Westenra
Subject: Serious stuff
Sent: June 20 5:18 AM

Lucy,

We're finally back! It's nice to be around real doctors and not Romanian nuns. They wore these old fashioned wimples with a top like a pillbox hat and a point under their chins like something from another century (a bad century). So, I'm sitting in this whitewashed room with a stone floor (it really WAS just like a nunnery from the movies) and this old lady with a face wrinkled up like a dried apricot comes in.

Nun: He is well, child.

Me (thinking he looks terrible and I can't wait to get him to a real hospital with beeping machines and guys in lab coats with stethoscopes): Thank you.

Nun: We have cast it out. The taint is gone.

Me (pretty impressed by her English but confused): Taint?

Nun: If he dies now (!!), he'll be innocent and pure.

I just stared at her with my mouth open, and then she said a prayer (in Latin, I think) and wandered off.

Getting him back was hard. We had to dope him up so much to keep him from yelling, we had to practically carry him on and off the plane. We had this same exchange about fifty times, but here's the gist of it:

J: It was full of skulls. Baby skulls.

Me: There were no skulls. The police searched the Count's castle. It was empty. Everything is fine.

J: I'm sorry for what I did to you.

Me: You didn't do anything to me. I'm ok. Everything's ok.

Then he would squash my hand so hard that my fingers practically went to sleep.

I just kept talking to him like he was a little kid or a horse or something. His dad was no help at all. He was more upset than I was.

But we're here now, and Jonathan's doctors say that he has "idiopathic autoimmune hemolytic anemia." Plus his psychological problems. As if those weren't enough.

He is super pale and has huge dark circles under his eyes. He looks like crap.

I'm scared.

Will tell you when I learn more. He's coming out now. Gotta run.

Call if you can. I need somebody sane. And you know how bad things are if I'm expecting YOU to be the sane one.

xoxo,
Mina

- - - - - - - - - - - - - - -Attachment Below- - - - - - - - - - - - - - -

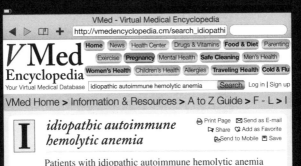

VMed - Virtual Medical Encyclopedia

http://vmedencyclopedia.cm/search_idiopathi

_V_Med
Encyclopedia
Your Virtual Medical Database

Home | News | Health Center | Drugs & Vitamins | **Food & Diet** | Parenting
Exercise | **Pregnancy** | Mental Health | **Safe Cleaning** | Men's Health
Women's Health | Children's Health | Allergies | **Traveling Health** | **Cold & Flu**

idiopathic autoimmune hemolytic anemia | Search | Log in | Sign up

VMed Home **>** Information & Resources **>** A to Z Guide **>** F - L **>** I

I *idiopathic autoimmune hemolytic anemia*

🖨 Print Page ✉ Send as E-mail
↪ Share ♥ Add as Favorite
📲 Send to Mobile 💾 Save

Patients with idiopathic autoimmune hemolytic anemia suffer a drop in the number of red blood cells. Causes for the disease are unknown (as evidenced by the word "idiopathic"), but it is considered an autoimmune disorder.

The symptoms include, as might be expected, dark urine, an enlarged spleen, fatigue, pallor, rapid heartbeat, shortness of breath, and jaundice.

The first-line treatment for idiopathic autoimmune hemolytic anemia is, of course, steroids, such as prednisone.

If the condition does not respond to steroids, a splenectomy (removal of the spleen) may be indicated.

If both of these avenues fail, immunosuppressive therapy is usually given, including administration of azathioprine, cyclophosphamide, and rituximab.

Blood transfusions are not recommended, as incompatible blood may cause further hemolysis.

Complications include infection and severe anemia.

iD

From: Mina Murray
To: Lucy Westenra
Subject: More serious stuff
Sent: June 20 6:23 AM

Lucy,

They are rushing Jonathan into surgery to remove his spleen. Usually they try steroids, but they say there's not time.

His mother is trying to get in from Canada for the surgery, but I don't think she'll make it. His father is here but useless. Still a mess.

The surgeons say he's super weak. I don't think they are hopeful about his recovery. But I'm trying to be.

Please call me. I need you. Besides Jonathan, you're my best friend.

What if I lose him, Lucy?

Mina

- - - - - - - - - - - - - - - -Attachment Below- - - - - - - - - - - - - - - -

VMed - Virtual Medical Encyclopedia

◀ ▶ 🖽 + http://vmedencyclopedia.cm/search_what-is-

*V*Med

Home | News | Health Center | Drugs & Vitamins | **Food & Diet** | Parenting

Exercise | **Pregnancy** | Mental Health | **Safe Cleaning** | Men's Health

Women's Health | Children's Health | Allergies | **Traveling Health** | **Cold & Flu**

Encyclopedia

Your Virtual Medical Database | what is a splenectomy? | Search | Log in | Sign up

VMed Home **>** Definitions **>** General Surgery **>** Splenectomy

 *Splenectomy:*A splenectomy is the surgical removal of the spleen.

🖨 Print Page ✉ Send as E-mail
↳ Share ☆ Add as Favorite
📱Send to Mobile 💾 Save

What does your spleen do?

Your spleen filters your blood by removing old red blood cells and platelets. The spleen also creates new blood cells and helps to fight off disease.

Can you live without a spleen?

Yes.

What are the complications of a splenectomy?

Most splenectomies have few complications.

But in a few cases the patient can contract an overwhelming bacterial infection after surgery. After two years, this risk goes way down.

Other very rare complications include inflammation of the pancreas, collapse of the lungs, and excessive bleeding.

iD

June 20 8:12 AM

J got thru ok. So far

June 20 8:15 AM

Lucy?

June 20 8:18 AM

U there?

From: Abraham Van Helsing
To: Mina Murray
Subject: Re: Delicate question
Sent: June 20 1:56 PM

Hello Mina,

I am sorry to report that Lucy is gravely ill. She was brought by ambulance to Lenox Hill Hospital Manhattan. She asks me to contact you.

She has acute idiopathic autoimmune hemolytic anemia. It is a very rare disorder, but they say it is almost never life threatening. She is being treated aggressively with steroids, and her doctors are cautiously hopeful.

I wish that there were another way to deliver the news to you, but I do not have your telephone number and Lucy is in no condition to tell it to me. Please contact me immediately. My number is 212-555-0184.

Abe

From:	Abraham Van Helsing
To:	Mina Murray
Subject:	Re: Delicate question
Sent:	June 20 7:29 PM

Hello Mina,

I would have called had I your number. Lucy's condition is critical.

Her family is at her bedside. I do not believe that she will last the night. We are at Lenox Hill Hospital Manhattan. Please come at once.

I am truly sorry to be the bearer of such sad tidings.

Abe

June 21 6:30 AM

Just woke up. Dad says Lucy
is really sick too. Call me.
URGENT

From: Mina Murray
To: Jonathan Harker
Subject: Lucy just died
Sent: June 21 7:29 AM

J,

Lucy just died. I'm crying so hard I can barely type. I would call you, but I don't want to talk to you. I can't believe that you slept with her. And that you had to tell me while she was dying.

I told her doctors about how you and Lucy have the same weird disease and about you and her. They said they would look into it.

Her father gave me that stuffed kitten she used to sleep with. Remember Mr. Bubbles? I'm going to put him in her coffin. I can't bear to think of her all alone in that box.

I'm going home to bed. Please don't call me. I don't want to talk to you.

M

The Gotham Times Online | Obits

www.gothamtimes.cm/us/regional/obits/Lucy_Westenra

Get Home Delivery | Log in | Register Now

The Gotham Times

U.S.

Search all Gotham Times Online [ ] Go

HOME PAGE | TODAY'S NEWS | VIDEOS | MOST POPULAR | GOTHAM TOPICS

WORLD | U.S. | REGION | BUSINESS | TECHNOLOGY | SCIENCE | HEALTH | SPORTS | OPINION | ARTS | STYLE | TRAVEL

POLITICS   EDUCATION   BAY AREA   CHICAGO

Obituaries

Lucy Westenra

WESTENRA—Lucy Ann, beloved daughter of prominent businessman Lawrence Westenra and his late wife, Lila Smith Westenra, died suddenly on June 21. Donations in her honor may be made to the National Organization for Rare Disorders.

Gotham's Top News
Daily E-Mail Alerts

Sign up for a grouping of the day's top stories, sent to your inbox every morning!

[ ] Sign Up

See Sample | Privacy Policy

✔ SIGN IN TO
RECOMMEND

✚ SHARE

✉ SIGN IN TO
E-MAIL

🖶 PRINT

🖨 REPRINTS

iD

From: Andrew Peterson
To: Abraham Van Helsing
Subject: A break?
Sent: June 24 8:18 AM

Abe,

This is a difficult email for me to write.

You have been a great asset during your time here, and I appreciate your hard work. You've been hit hard by the death of the woman you were seeing and understandably so, but your behavior has become inexcusably erratic. You must stay away from Randolph Renfield. Your presence agitates him, and your questioning him about his psychosis as if it were real is not helping him any. I have warned you several times, but I keep hearing that you are in his room on all of your breaks.

Remember that your girlfriend's death was not your fault. Nor was it Randolph Renfield's. Her condition was untreatable and fast advancing. No one could have helped her. When you become a doctor, you will have to deal with this kind of situation far too often.

Please consider taking some time off. We will be assigning your duties to another volunteer for a few weeks.

Things don't always happen for a reason. Sometimes they just happen.

If you ever need someone to listen, I'm here for you. Heck, I'm even trained for it.

Stop by my office when you get this so we can discuss. Please.

Andy

From: Mina Murray
To: Abraham Van Helsing
Subject: Can we meet?
Sent: June 24 8:25 AM

Abe,

Thank you for the things you said about Lucy. I think you understood her essence—generous, loving, and full of life—better than many who knew her longer.

I hate to ask this, but could we meet? Jonathan, my boyfriend, is ill, with acute idiopathic autoimmune hemolytic anemia: same as what killed Lucy. No one knows how they got it: environmental, close contact, or a giant coincidence. The day that she died, Jonathan confessed to me that he and Lucy slept together (not since your relationship with her started but well after ours did). If the disease is sexually transmitted, I worry that you and I might have been exposed. Is there a way to test for it? I told Lucy's doctors, but they didn't take me seriously.

I'm sorry to give you more bad news, but I thought you'd want to know. Jonathan is slowly recovering, so I guess the splenectomy was a better cure than the steroids they gave Lucy. As tragic as it is, that knowledge may end up saving our lives if we do catch what they had.

Please call me as soon as you can.
Mina

From:	Mina Murray
To:	info@nybloodcenter.org
Subject:	Problem with my blood
Sent:	June 24 9:30 AM

Hello,

The blood I donated at the charity ball in Manhattan on June 16 may be tainted. I just found out that I may have been exposed to a fatal blood-borne disease that presented itself as acute idiopathic autoimmune hemolytic anemia. I called and spoke to a Dr. Seward about it, and I am sending this email as a follow-up. If you still have my blood, please destroy it. If you have transfused it into someone else, please refer them to Dr. Seward.

Thank you, and I am deeply, deeply sorry. I never would have donated blood if I had known.

Sincerely,

Mina Murray

From: Jonathan Harker
To: Mina Murray
Subject: I'm so sorry
Sent: June 24 11:38 AM

Darling Mina,

I am so sorry for what I've put you through. I hated to tell you about my fling with Lucy, but I knew you needed to know in case I exposed you to something. It was just a few times, and I don't think it meant anything to her either. I know it was wrong, and if you give me another chance, I can be the man that you always thought I was.

I love you, Mina. It took all this for me to realize it. Stupid, I know.

You have always been my foundation. Without you I feel like I'm sinking in quicksand. I need you, and more than I ever appreciated.

I understand why you don't want to take my calls, but please reconsider. The doctors aren't sure how to fix what's wrong with me, and I would hate to leave this world with you hating me.

Would write longer but am weak today. Am having trouble with the keyboard on Dad's laptop. My laptop and phone disappeared in Romania. I think I threw them into a river. I know that sounds crazy.

I know I can never make it right, but please please please let me try.

Yours,
J

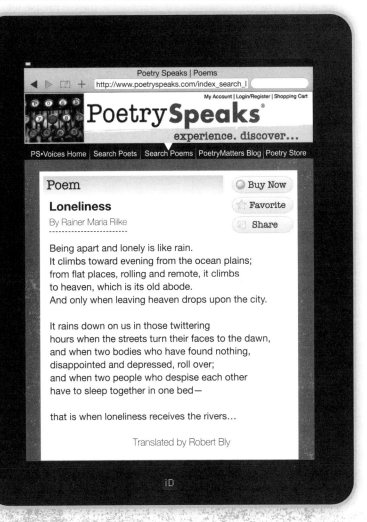

Poetry Speaks | Poems

http://www.poetryspeaks.com/index_search_l

My Account | Login/Register | Shopping Cart

Poetry **Speaks**®

experience. discover...

PS•Voices Home | Search Poets | Search Poems | PoetryMatters Blog | Poetry Store

Poem

Buy Now

Favorite

Share

Loneliness

By Rainer Maria Rilke

Being apart and lonely is like rain.
It climbs toward evening from the ocean plains;
from flat places, rolling and remote, it climbs
to heaven, which is its old abode.
And only when leaving heaven drops upon the city.

It rains down on us in those twittering
hours when the streets turn their faces to the dawn,
and when two bodies who have found nothing,
disappointed and depressed, roll over;
and when two people who despise each other
have to sleep together in one bed—

that is when loneliness receives the rivers...

Translated by Robert Bly

iD

From: Abraham Van Helsing
To: Mina Murray
Subject: Re: Can we meet?
Sent: June 24 12:10 PM

Mina,

I left a message on your cell phone but thought perhaps I should email you as well.

I would be happy to meet at your earliest convenience. Sexually transmitted anemia seems unlikely, but anemia can also be a symptom of other diseases, some of which are sexually transmitted (such as HIV, but I know that Lucy tested negative for that, so please put your mind at rest on that score).

I think that you and I should go to the same lab to be tested. One of my professors is also a hematologist, so I should be able to put together a list of specialists we can consult.

So far, I have had no symptoms, and I understand that you do not either? Try not to worry yourself too much. We will do what we can and see.

I'm sorry that you are having to deal with all this on top of Lucy's death, Mina.

Abe

From:	Mina Murray
To:	Jonathan Harker
Subject:	Re: I'm so sorry
Sent:	June 24 4:04 PM

Jonathan,

I don't hate you. I also don't want to see you right now. I know the timing is bad for you. It isn't great for me either. Next time you sleep around, maybe YOU should worry about the timing.

Abe recommended that you make a list of your sexual partners for the past year, in case you exposed them, too. Hope you don't get writer's cramp.

Not that you care, but we stopped by to see Renfield. Abe is going to take blood samples from all of us to compare with yours and Lucy's to see if there are any matches. Plus I wanted to see Renfield again, and Abe didn't want me to go in by myself since Renfield bit Lucy last time. Abe actually didn't want me to go in the room with Renfield at all (he's a kinda protective guy), but I insisted (I'm a kinda persistent girl).

Renfield was calmer than last time, but instead of yelling he cried. He was in a strait jacket after attacking Lucy. It seems so long ago now, but it has only been a week. Here's what he said (I'm only telling you because he mentioned you):

Renfield: I am sorry for what I did to Lucy Westenra. For what he did to Lucy Westenra.

Me: Who?

Renfield: The Master. I am sorry for what he did to Jonathan Harker. But he is healed, isn't he? The Master cannot find Jonathan Harker anymore, so he is dead or still alive. But healed.

Me (getting sick to my stomach, thinking of those nuns): Healed of what?

Renfield: You know, Mina Murray, even if you pretend you do not. Tell Jonathan Harker that I beg his forgiveness, as I will beg forgiveness of Lucy Westenra when I see her.

Me: Lucy is... (and I just couldn't tell him, but I started to cry, so the jig was pretty much up).

Renfield: You think she is dead, but she is not. We moved beyond death, she and I. But it was not like I thought.

He looked around like he expected something to come through the walls. He trembled so hard his teeth chattered. Then he hid under his bed. After I coaxed him out, Abe asked for a blood sample.

Renfield went ballistic. He said that he had worked so hard to make his blood strong that he couldn't spare even a single drop. He had to be sedated again, but Abe took his blood sample. Is that even legal, taking someone's blood against his will like that? I don't know, but we do need it.

In spite of everything, I hope you feel better soon. I will talk to you as soon as I feel up to it. Which might be a while.

Mina
- - - - - - - - - - - - - - -Attachment Below- - - - - - - - - - - - - -

From: Jonathan Harker
To: Mina Murray
Subject: Re: I'm so sorry
Sent: June 24 4:07 PM

Dearest Mina,

Thank you for writing me back. It's more than I deserve, and I know that.

I will make that list and pass it along to Van Helsing. Send me his email address.

I know Renfield is crazy. But did you see that article about the bat attacks near the cemetery where Lucy is buried? Probably a coincidence, but when I read about it my eyes actually went dark and I thought I would pass out. You know I'm not a drama queen about being sick, but I think all of this ties into the hallucinations I had in Romania.

Maybe they were true. Maybe the Count is a killer. And I feel much weaker today than ever before.

What if Renfield is right?

What happened to Lucy's body? Please tell me she was cremated.

But I don't think she was. In my heart, I feel like Lucy is out there somewhere waiting for me.

And it scares the hell out of me. Will I end up killing children like the Count?

I have no right to ask this, but could you please visit me? I feel so alone.

J

From: Mina Murray
To: Jonathan Harker
Subject: Re: I'm so sorry
Sent: June 24 4:28 PM

Jonathan,

>I will make that list and pass it along to Van Helsing.

There is a list!?! Not just Lucy? How many others?

Were you ever faithful to me? Was I wrong about all of it? Every single minute?

Don't tell me. I don't even want to know.

I certainly will NOT visit you. And you should count yourself lucky that I won't.

Mina

From: Jonathan Harker
To: Mina Murray
Subject: Re: I'm so sorry
Sent: June 24 4:44 PM

Dearest Mina,

I know I've acted unforgivably. And I'd like to spend a lifetime making it up to you. Don't overreact. What we have is very special. Every minute is not a lie. There is profound truth there, even if I didn't realize it until now.

I'm not going to ask you to forgive me. Just please let me back in. We can rebuild our relationship stronger now that it's been through the fire.

Please. And please also be careful with the Count. Please tell me what's going on there. It's the least you can do. Remember, my neck is on the line, too.

Love,
J

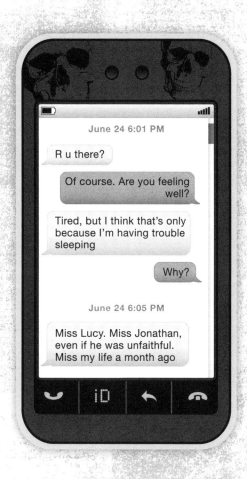

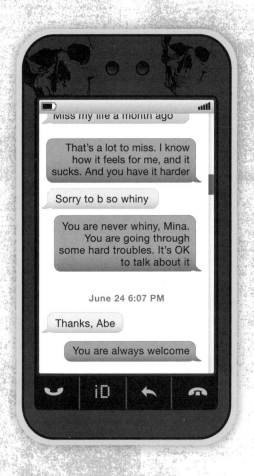

Miss my life a month ago

That's a lot to miss. I know how it feels for me, and it sucks. And you have it harder

Sorry to b so whiny

You are never whiny, Mina. You are going through some hard troubles. It's OK to talk about it

June 24 6:07 PM

Thanks, Abe

You are always welcome

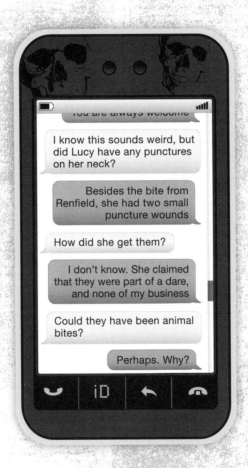

You are always welcome

I know this sounds weird, but did Lucy have any punctures on her neck?

Besides the bite from Renfield, she had two small puncture wounds

How did she get them?

I don't know. She claimed that they were part of a dare, and none of my business

Could they have been animal bites?

Perhaps. Why?

Perhaps. Why?

Recent bat attacks in the cemetery where Lucy is buried. Lucy used to go there to visit her mother's grave

Bats can harbor certain diseases. I will look into it

Thanks

Take care of yourself, Mina

u 2

From: Jonathan Hayes
To: Abraham Van Helsing
Subject: Autopsy attached
Sent: June 25 10:26 AM

Abe,

Let me repeat my condolences at your loss. I understand why you are trying to keep yourself occupied, but maybe a break would be best. Trust me, you don't want to push yourself too hard. Been there, done that.

That said, I'm attaching an autopsy report of one of the attack victims that you requested. I look forward to seeing you in class again next fall.

Call me.

Jon

Office of Chief Medical Examiner
City of New York
Report of Autopsy

Name of Decedent: Unknown White Male

M.E. Case #: 666-666

Autopsy Performed by: Dr. Jonathan Hayes

Date of Autopsy: June 23

AUTOPSY FINDINGS

I. EXSANGUINATION DUE TO PUNCTURE WOUNDS OF NECK:

    A. PAIRED PUNCTURE WOUNDS LEFT LATERAL NECK WITH JUGULAR VEIN PUNCTURES:

        1. MINIMAL LOCAL SOFT TISSUE BLEEDING.

    B. ABSENT LIVOR MORTIS.

    C. GENERALIZED VISCERAL PALLOR.

    D. NO FREE BLOOD IN VESSELS.

    E. FINDINGS CONSISTENT WITH HYPOVOLEMIC SHOCK, INCLUDING SUBENDOCARDIAL

HEMORRHAGE IN LEFT VENTRICULAR
OUTFLOW AND MUCOSAL HEMORRHAGES OF
THE RENAL PELVIS.

F.   SHRINKAGE OF SPLEEN.

CAUSE OF DEATH: EXSANGUINATION DUE TO
PUNCTURE WOUNDS OF NECK.

MANNER OF DEATH: HOMICIDE.

OFFICE OF CHIEF MEDICAL EXAMINER

I hereby certify that I, Jonathan Hayes, M.D.,
New York City Medical Examiner, have performed an
autopsy on the body of **Unknown White Male,** on the
23rd day of June, commencing at 1:00 p.m., in the New
York City Mortuary of the Office of Chief Medical
Examiner.

EXTERNAL EXAMINATION:

The decedent is initially viewed clad in a dark
gray sleeveless T-shirt style top, blue jeans and
belt, gray sweat shorts and socks. A right eyebrow
piercing with indwelling white metal barbell stud is
in place. A navel piercing in white metal is present.
The body jewelry is left in place and secured with
evidence tape.

The body is that of a well-developed, well-nourished,

slender, 5' 7", approximately 120 lbs, White male whose appearance is consistent with an age in the mid-late teens. Muscular rigidity is moderate and symmetric and lividity is completely absent in the cool body; the body is strikingly pale.

EVIDENCE OF MEDICAL INTERVENTION: NONE

EVIDENCE OF INJURY: PUNCTURE WOUNDS OF NECK:
On the left lateral neck at a point 8" below the top of the head and 2 1/2" to the left of the midline, situated in the mid-region of the anterior border of the left sternomastoid muscle, there are two circular, punctate defects approximately 1/4" in diameter. The wounds are symmetric, identical in appearance; it cannot be determined whether the wounding implement consists of a weapon with a double tip, such as a barbecue fork, or whether the injuries represent two separate wounds with a single-tipped weapon with a slender, pointed weapon, such as an ice pick.

A near-bloodless wound track is noted extending into the soft tissues of the neck for a total depth of approximately 1", penetrating both the internal and external jugular veins on the left side of the neck; there are multiple overlapping defects in both veins, suggesting multiple incomplete withdrawals of the weapon before it was thrust back in again.

The surrounding tissues are nearly bloodless, with minimal extravasation of blood. The lack of damage to the tissues and surrounding skin, and the presence of only two defects makes it unlikely that the injury represents an animal bite; however, swabs were taken of the skin surface and submitted for DNA/forensic biology analysis in the customary manner.

The decedent is effectively bloodless; the body has no lividity, and there is no free blood in the vessels, including the aorta and vena cavae. The viscera are strikingly pale, as is the brain, and there is subendocardial hemorrhage in the left ventricular outflow tract and mucosal petechiae in the renal pelvic mucosa, consistent with terminal hypovolemic shock. By X-ray, there is no retained foreign body in the neck. There is no evidence of cardiac air embolism.

From:	Mina Murray
To:	Jonathan Harker
Subject:	Re: I'm so sorry
Sent:	June 25 3:52 PM

Jonathan,

We have started to investigate ourselves. Here is your status report.

Step 1: Get autopsy report from one of the victims of the attacks near the cemetery where Lucy and her mother are buried.

Abe got one. Cause of death: massive blood loss. Only wound: two punctures in the neck. Someone or something is puncturing their necks and draining their blood. They are dying from loss of blood.

Step 2: Get into crypt.

I visited Lucy's father. He's a mess. First his wife and now his daughter. I sat with him for about an hour. I don't know if he'll get through this. I'm going to keep checking in on him. It seemed to help, at least a little, but it's so hard to see how broken he is now.

He loaned me the key to Lucy's crypt. I didn't tell him why I needed it, and he didn't ask.

Step 3: See if Lucy's body is still there. I know, it's crazy, so don't lecture me.

Abe and I met in front of the crypt, by the marble lamb. It's where I used to meet Lucy. I went there so many times with her visiting her mother's grave that I half expected her to show up. But she didn't.

Just like Lucy used to do, I unlocked that green metal door, and Abe and I stepped in. It was warm and stuffy inside, and it smelled terrible, like death. All the flowers that went in there after the funeral were dead and brown.

We had to leave the door open to let it air out. I tried not to think about how it must be Lucy making that smell. Lucy, my best friend since kindergarten. It didn't feel real, but it is.

Abe brought a crowbar, but when we got to her coffin, we froze for a long time. (I mean, breaking open a coffin? I've never done anything like that before. What if we got arrested? What if I had to see her body again and it was all rotted? It all felt so wrong and sad and messed up.)

If it had been me, I would have left. But not Abe. He is a man of action.

He broke open her coffin.

It was empty. No Lucy and no Mr. Bubbles.

The logical explanation is that someone stole her body, which is creepy enough, but...if someone took her body, why did they take Mr. Bubbles, too?

In the back of the crypt, where the really old bodies are, we found a large box made out of a black wood and filled with dirt. Remember the ebony boxes the Count had you ship from Romania?

Mina

- - - - - - - - - - - - - - -Attachment Below- - - - - - - - - - - - - - -

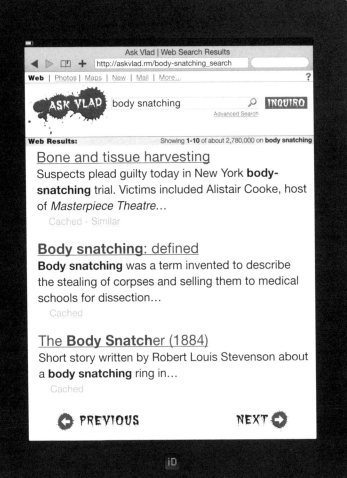

Ask Vlad | Web Search Results

http://askvlad.rm/body-snatching_search

Web | Photos | Maps | New | Mail | More...

ASK VLAD   body snatching   **INQUIRO**

Advanced Search

Web Results: Showing **1-10** of about 2,780,000 on **body snatching**

Bone and tissue harvesting

Suspects plead guilty today in New York **body-snatching** trial. Victims included Alistair Cooke, host of *Masterpiece Theatre*...

Cached - Similar

Body snatching: defined

Body snatching was a term invented to describe the stealing of corpses and selling them to medical schools for dissection...

Cached

The **Body Snatch**er (1884)

Short story written by Robert Louis Stevenson about a **body snatching** ring in...

Cached

◀ **PREVIOUS**   **NEXT** ▶

iD

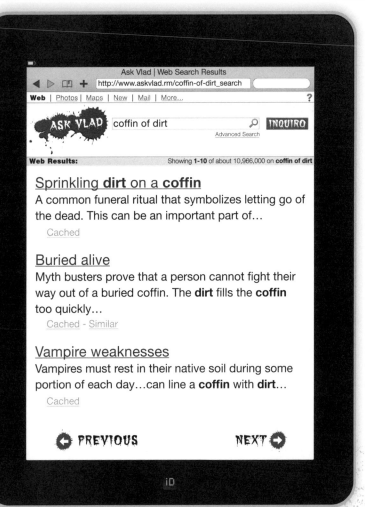

Ask Vlad | Web Search Results

◄ ▷ ▢ + http://www.askvlad.rm/coffin-of-dirt_search

Web | Photos | Maps | New | Mail | More...   ?

ASK VLAD coffin of dirt   🔍 **INQUIRO**
                                          Advanced Search

Web Results: Showing **1-10** of about 10,966,000 on **coffin of dirt**

Sprinkling **dirt** on a **coffin**
A common funeral ritual that symbolizes letting go of
the dead. This can be an important part of…
   Cached

Buried alive
Myth busters prove that a person cannot fight their
way out of a buried coffin. The **dirt** fills the **coffin**
too quickly…
   Cached - Similar

Vampire weaknesses
Vampires must rest in their native soil during some
portion of each day…can line a **coffin** with **dirt**…
   Cached

○ PREVIOUS   **NEXT ○**

iD

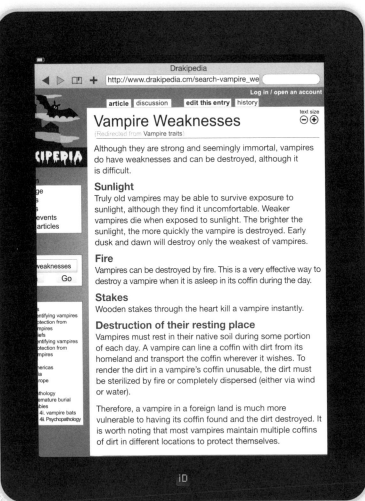

Drakipedia

◀ ▶ ▭ ＋ http://www.drakipedia.cm/search-vampire_we

Log in / open an account

article discussion **edit this entry** history

CIPEDIA

Vampire Weaknesses

(Redirected from Vampire traits)

text size
⊖⊕

Although they are strong and seemingly immortal, vampires do have weaknesses and can be destroyed, although it is difficult.

Sunlight

Truly old vampires may be able to survive exposure to sunlight, although they find it uncomfortable. Weaker vampires die when exposed to sunlight. The brighter the sunlight, the more quickly the vampire is destroyed. Early dusk and dawn will destroy only the weakest of vampires.

Fire

Vampires can be destroyed by fire. This is a very effective way to destroy a vampire when it is asleep in its coffin during the day.

Stakes

Wooden stakes through the heart kill a vampire instantly.

Destruction of their resting place

Vampires must rest in their native soil during some portion of each day. A vampire can line a coffin with dirt from its homeland and transport the coffin wherever it wishes. To render the dirt in a vampire's coffin unusable, the dirt must be sterilized by fire or completely dispersed (either via wind or water).

Therefore, a vampire in a foreign land is much more vulnerable to having its coffin found and the dirt destroyed. It is worth noting that most vampires maintain multiple coffins of dirt in different locations to protect themselves.

iD

From: Mina Murray
To: Jonathan Harker
Subject: Re: I'm so sorry
Sent: June 25 7:26 PM

Jonathan,

Abe hired some guys to take out the box, and we took a boat into the harbor and dumped the dirt into the ocean (yes, we had to pay them extra as it's illegal apparently). Afterward we burned the box and scattered the ashes. Some sources say that a vampire must sleep in the soil of his native land to regenerate. I know I've gone beyond crazy. It's all adrenaline and insanity now.

When you get this, call me. I need the address of the house the Count bought in Manhattan. We're going to see if it has the other two dirt boxes.

I know, it all sounds super nuts and probably is. But, if I'm wrong, what harm can there be in throwing away dirt? (except for the illegal part and also that we're clearly stealing it, so delete this email)

Call.

Mina
- - - - - - - - - - - - - - -Attachment Below- - - - - - - - - - - - - - -

June 25 8:07 PM

Can we meet at the lab?

Of course

I have the count's manhattan address

You are amazing!

I wish

It is true, Mina

June 25 8:09 PM

C u soon

From: Mina Murray
To: Jonathan Harker
Subject: Re: I'm so sorry
Sent: June 26 2:41 PM

Jonathan,

It was good to hear your voice, but you sound terrible. I'm sorry I cried on the phone. It's been hard losing Lucy and then you. Except for Abe, I'm all alone. I miss the Three Musketeers. Here's your status report. It's all I can give you right now:

Abe and I went to that address. Door was locked. But Abe called a locksmith who was only too happy to break us in. He didn't even ask for ID! Abe is really most amazing. I was a nervous wreck. I'm such a goody-goody at the weirdest times.

Inside we found no trace of the Count, but we did find another box of dirt. We had it hauled off and dumped it in the harbor like last time. (expensive!) Whatever the Count was using it for, that's over. There is only one box left. I don't know if we could afford more. We both had to stop by the ATM to get enough for this round. There goes months of baby-sitting money. I thought of asking Mom for money, but how can I possibly explain why I need it?

I don't know what to believe anymore but am acting on faith. What disease do you have? Did the nuns really cure you? Where are Lucy's body and Mr. Bubbles? Where is the Count? What killed Lucy?

Just found out that Renfield died last night. I called his father, which was just as terrible as you can imagine. But it was the right thing to do. You should call him, too. I know you probably won't, but you should. Be prepared for him to cry into the phone. And try to suck it up and not cry yourself. I managed but have had a stomachache ever since.

According to the attendants, Renfield talked to himself just before he died using two different voices. One voice begged the other voice for something, and the other voice was angry. The attendants weren't worried about it. (What would worry them, I wonder?)

Around midnight there was a tremendous banging and crashing. The attendants rushed to check. When they unlocked the door, Renfield was lying in a pool of blood, barely alive.

He was alone in a locked room, so they think he had some kind of fit. They think he smashed himself against the wall a couple of times, then somehow managed to fall out of bed and break his back. (like that sounds logical)

Before Renfield died, he told the attendants the following:

Renfield: Tell Abe Van Helsing that he must find the last box. He must destroy it, to destroy the Count and Lucy and to set me free. Kill the master and the undead fledglings die; the living fledglings are released.

How could Renfield even know about the dirt? Unless the Count knows and told him.

And it's that "unless" that scares me. But Abe is remarkably brave, and I'm sharing his courage. My courage comes and goes. Right now: courage = gone.

Mina

From: Jonathan Harker
To: Mina Murray
Subject: Re: I'm so sorry
Sent: June 26 5:13 PM

Mina,

I am glad that you are corresponding with me at all. It's a lot.

I wish I could get out of this damn hospital bed to help you. But my energy level is so low that I need help to get to the bathroom. I have faith in you though. I always knew you were strong, but I didn't realize how incredibly strong until this happened. You are doing better on your own than you ever did with me.

If anyone can do this, you can. You brought me home from Romania. Dad says you practically did it single-handedly.

Know that I'm always here for you. No matter what happens.

I love you.

J

June 27 2:13 AM

R u awake?

What's wrong?

Woke up with a bite mark on my neck. I'm afraid to tell Abe

What happened?

Not sure. I was fine when I went to bed

But?

But I dreamed that someone got into my room

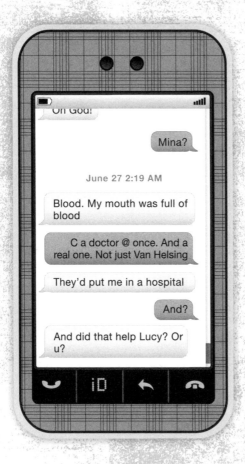

Oh God!

Mina?

June 27 2:19 AM

Blood. My mouth was full of blood

C a doctor @ once. And a real one. Not just Van Helsing

They'd put me in a hospital

And?

And did that help Lucy? Or u?

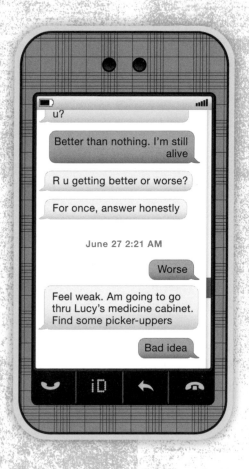

From: Abraham Van Helsing
To: Mina Murray
Subject: Call me, please
Sent: June 27 3:03 AM

Mina,

When you wake up, please call me and I will come and fetch you. I think we should not be separated from one another. No one should die alone as Renfield did. And, on a lighter note, I also miss you.

I could not sleep, so I went to the university laboratory. I have been checking our blood samples against normal and there is something wrong with the RBCs of Jonathan, Lucy, and Renfield. Not, thank God, with yours or mine yet.

I looked into bats for you. Blood-borne illnesses can be transmitted by bat bites, and not only rabies. In fact, it is now theorized that the Ebola virus lives in species of African fruit bats. They are called a reservoir species because they can carry the virus without immediately dying. Ebola is, of course, quickly fatal to humans (and a host of other mammals as well).

I wish I had a sample of one of the bats. And I still have no idea how the caskets of dirt fit in. Perhaps the Count has pet bats and they feed on something in the soil?

Or if we are willing to throw science to the wind: Renfield is right and we are dealing with something that can't be cured by scientific means.

Call me, please.

Returning to my microscope,
Abe

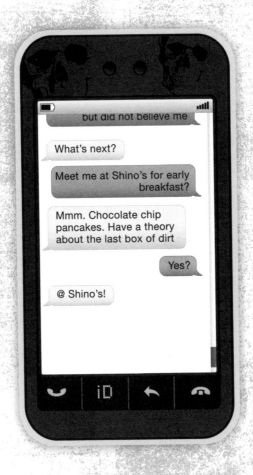

but did not believe me

What's next?

Meet me at Shino's for early breakfast?

Mmm. Chocolate chip pancakes. Have a theory about the last box of dirt

Yes?

@ Shino's!

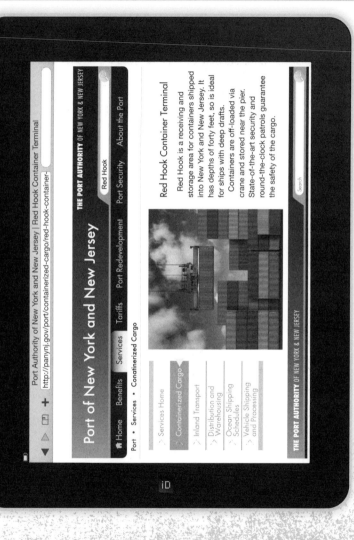

Port Authority of New York and New Jersey | Red Hook Container Terminal

http://panynj.gov/port/containerized-cargo/red-hook-container-

Port of New York and New Jersey

THE PORT AUTHORITY OF NEW YORK & NEW JERSEY

🏠 Home   Benefits   **Services**   Tariffs   Port Redevelopment   Port Security   About the Port

Red Hook

Port • Services • Containerized Cargo

> Services Home
> **Containerized Cargo**
> Inland Transport
> Distribution and Warehousing
> Ocean Shipping Schedules
> Vehicle Shipping and Processing

Red Hook Container Terminal

Red Hook is a receiving and storage area for containers shipped into New York and New Jersey. It has depths of forty feet, so is ideal for ships with deep drafts.

Containers are off-loaded via crane and stored near the pier. State-of-the-art security and round-the-clock patrols guarantee the safety of the cargo.

THE PORT AUTHORITY OF NEW YORK & NEW JERSEY

ASK VLAD

▲ ▼ ⊞ + http://www.askvlad.rm/Times-of-sunrise-and-sunset-in-ny-Jun

Ask Vlad | Image Search Results

Times of sunrise and sunset in NY in June 🔍 INQUIRQ Back to results ⊠ Close search bar ?

June

New York, New York Sunrises and Sunsets

Sunday	Monday	Tuesday	Wednesday	Thursday	Friday	Saturday
	1 Sunrise: 5:26am Sunset: 8:20pm	2 Sunrise: 5:26am Sunset: 8:21pm	3 Sunrise: 5:26am Sunset: 8:22pm	4 Sunrise: 5:25am Sunset: 8:22pm	5 Sunrise: 5:25am Sunset: 8:23pm	6 Sunrise: 5:25am Sunset: 8:24pm
7 Sunrise: 5:24am Sunset: 8:24pm	8 Sunrise: 5:24am Sunset: 8:25pm	9 Sunrise: 5:24am Sunset: 8:25pm	10 Sunrise: 5:24am Sunset: 8:26pm	11 Sunrise: 5:24am Sunset: 8:27pm	12 Sunrise: 5:24am Sunset: 8:27pm	13 Sunrise: 5:23am Sunset: 8:28pm
14 Sunrise: 5:23am Sunset: 8:28pm	15 Sunrise: 5:23am Sunset: 8:28pm	16 Sunrise: 5:23am Sunset: 8:29pm	17 Sunrise: 5:24am Sunset: 8:29pm	18 Sunrise: 5:24am Sunset: 8:30pm	19 Sunrise: 5:24am Sunset: 8:30pm	20 Sunrise: 5:24am Sunset: 8:30pm
21 Sunrise: 5:24am Sunset: 8:30pm	22 Sunrise: 5:24am Sunset: 8:31pm	23 Sunrise: 5:25am Sunset: 8:31pm	24 Sunrise: 5:25am Sunset: 8:31pm	25 Sunrise: 5:25am Sunset: 8:31pm	26 Sunrise: 5:26am Sunset: 8:31pm	27 Sunrise: 5:26am Sunset: 8:31pm
28 Sunrise: 5:26am Sunset: 8:31pm	29 Sunrise: 5:27am Sunset: 8:31pm	30 Sunrise: 5:27am Sunset: 8:31pm				

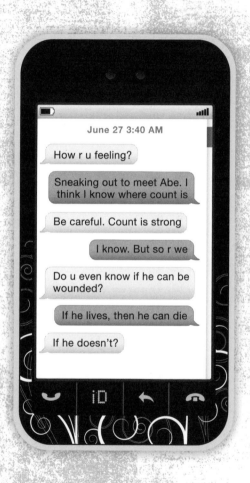

If he doesn't?

The books all say to drive a wooden stake through the heart. Or use fire

Listen to urself

U got something better?

June 27 3:41 AM

Just be careful. I luv u. Don't want to lose u

U didn't lose me. U threw me away

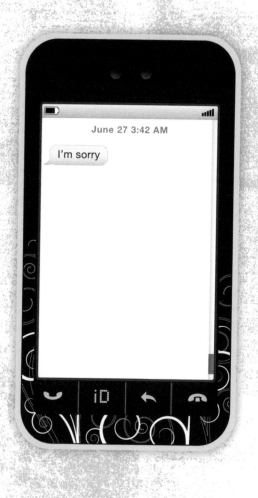

From: Mina Murray
To: Jonathan Harker
Subject: We're here
Sent: June 27 5:11 AM

Jonathan,

We stopped by the Count's Manhattan apartment on the way here (now that we have a key, it's not that hard). That place is HUGE. Last time I was so focused on getting out that box of dirt that I didn't notice.

Abe collected up all the shipping paperwork, so I looked up the container number there.

We snuck in at the docks. There were probably security cameras everywhere, but Abe cut a hole through a fence with bolt cutters and we crawled in.

The container is locked, but Abe's working on it with the bolt cutters. I'm being lookout.

We'll never get the box of dirt to the water in that amount of time. We'll have to burn it. It's just a matter of getting it done before the Count comes back or a security guard catches us. And not incinerating ourselves in the process.

Wish me luck.

Mina
- - - - - - - - - - - - - - -Attachment Below- - - - - - - - - - - - - - -

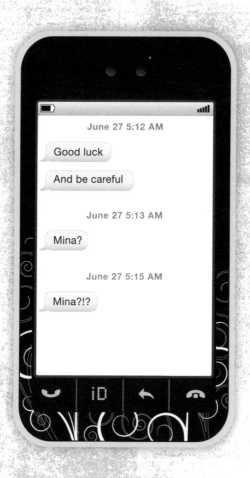

From: Mina Murray
To: Lucy Westenra
Subject: I'm sorry: Part I
Sent: June 27 7:28 PM

Lucy,

A lot has changed for me in such a short time. I'm not even sure what to say. But I know I owe you an explanation for what happened last night, even though I don't understand everything. Or anything, really.

We came looking for you and the Count, Abe and I. It was the middle of the night. We wanted to find and destroy the Count's last box of dirt and end the nightmare. I'd been bitten by that point, but I'm sure you know that. I wasn't fully turned, and I was sick and weak in a way I hope never to be again. I also had to hide it from Abe. You know how he is.

So we went to the yard and broke open the lock on the Count's container. That smell is terrible for...

I was going to write "humans." I guess that's right.

Abe threw up. He even swore in Dutch, which in spite of everything was kind of cute. Anyway, we had to wait for it to air out. A human frailty that cost us time.

Inside the container we found the last box of dirt. Near the top, where you must have rested your head, was Mr. Bubbles. That's when I started crying. I knew it meant that you were there. That you were a vampire. And that we would have to kill you. Hard to believe that a little stuffed kitten could mean so much.

But the security guard caught us. Officer Quincy Morris asked us to freeze and put our hands in the air.

Of course Abe and I did, being good citizens.

But you and the Count didn't, did you? I saw you rise up behind the security guy, past his car.

Abe crossed himself, as if that would have helped. I just stood there staring at you. You were both so terrible and fierce. But to tell the truth? You were beautiful, and I was grateful for a second that you were not dead.

His blood was in my veins, and it started to burn. So I knew it was real and I was in the middle of it and I might never get out. I was scared, but I was also grateful that I might be with you, like all my life, and you would lead me into trouble and out of it again.

That was when the security guy, Officer Morris, shot the Count. How can you blame him? He was scared out of his freaking mind. It didn't do anything, of course. The bullets just went right through him and pinged off the metal containers. I was scared out of my mind, too. Bullets still kill humans.

The Count put a stop to it. He grabbed the security guy and threw him into his windshield.

Officer Morris lay there like a sack. I almost sensed that he was dead then. I'd never seen anyone killed before. It wasn't grotesque or loud or even all that bloody, like it is in the movies. It just...was.

Abe grabbed my hand and pulled me away. We ran together. But even after all that, I wasn't sure that I wanted to run away from you two. I wanted to talk to you. To ask you how it was.

I have to go now. I just heard something. But I'll send you the next part soon.

Mina

- - - - - - - - - - - - - -Attachment Below- - - - - - - - - - - - - - -

From: Mina Murray
To: Lucy Westenra
Subject: I'm sorry: Part II
Sent: June 27 8:03 PM

Lucy,

I'm back. Nothing important. I think my senses are heightened. I'm on edge after last night.

Where was I? We were running.

Abe and I ducked behind Officer Morris's car. Abe wanted to get inside and drive off. Sensible man, Abe.

But you know what? I knew that if the Count got away I would become a vampire, like you. I was scared but not scared enough. Abe wanted to wait for full daylight, but I asked him to come with me right then so I didn't have to face you by myself. He took my hand, and we stood up together. The sun had already risen, and I saw you standing in the shadow of the Count's container. Abe and I were in the sunlight. I know you know this part, but I want you to see it through my eyes anyway.

Abe drew a circle around us with a piece of wood from his pocket and filled it up with liquid. He told me to stay in the circle but didn't explain why.

It didn't make sense to me. The only thing that made sense = you. My best friend was far from me and standing next to a vampire in the dawn in a godforsaken industrial wasteland.

I ignored Abe and I held up Mr. Bubbles for you to see. I wanted you to come take him back. I wanted to tempt you into the sunlight. You kept pacing back and forth in the shadow. I saw that you wanted him, but you were afraid. The Count just watched everything with his thousand-year-old smile.

Suddenly you did run across the sunlight to me. You looked at me and your eyes were gone. You didn't know me. But you've known me all your life. Then you looked at Mr. Bubbles and you really SAW him and for a second I thought everything would be all right again.

You grabbed Mr. Bubbles and I grabbed you. Abe lit the liquid and it blazed up and we were caught in the center of a ring of fire. You couldn't get out. The Count couldn't get in. And your eyes were gone again.

You were desperate. You always were, though. I thought you would kill me then, but I held you still enough for Abe to get out his stake. He tried to drive it in, but he wasn't strong enough.

By then you were suffering and screaming and I knew I had to end it. I didn't want to. You might have been strong, but you were broken and hurting. I could feel how angry the Count was. He and I thought the same thing: you couldn't be mended.

So, I helped Abe.

The stake went in and you looked so surprised. But the screaming stopped. You just stared at me as if you'd never seen me before. Never believed that I could do something like that. Even to save my own life.

I never thought I could either.

Then the charred ring spread out around the stake. That black nothingness radiated around it until you were gone. I was staring at the spot where you were. Abe was crying, and I was crying.

I'm crying again while I type this. I'll be back as soon as I can and tell you all the things you didn't see.

Love,
Mina

From: Mina Murray
To: Lucy Westenra
Subject: I'm sorry: Part III
Sent: June 27 10:13 PM

I'll finish it all in this email. I promise.

I heard the Count snap his fingers. He said, "Enough, Mina. Come!"

I turned and stepped right through the flames to go to him. I couldn't stop myself; I had no power to do anything else. His blood in my body did what it was told. I didn't even think of struggling.

Abe ran after me and yelled my name. I could barely hear him. It was like I was underwater. The Count said that I was his.

Foolhardy Abe jumped between us. He pulled a stake out of his back pocket and he held it up to me. For a second I thought he was going to try to stake me like we did with you. But you know what? I wasn't even worried. I knew that he couldn't really hurt me, not by himself with the Count's blood in me and him right there.

Turns out Abe couldn't try. He lowered the stake. Tears ran down his face, and he just said, "I cannot hurt you."

The Count laughed, "How I adore a human in love. Wonderfully predictable."

I felt bad for Abe because he didn't understand anything.

When I reached down to take his hand I found the stake instead, so I put it in my pocket. The Count grabbed him and threw him inside the container. Abe landed hard. A gross thud of bones and flesh...I didn't know if he was dead or alive.

That snapped me out of it. I was scared then. The Count might do anything to me, too. My neck started bleeding again. He led me into the terrible container, and I was shaking. I've never been so afraid in my life.

The Count knew how scared I was. He took me in his arms and he kissed me, and I was gone, gone, gone. I'd never felt anything like it. Everything vanished and it was just the Count and me and his lips and this feeling of warmth and contentment and waves and waves of pleasure washing over me and I wanted it to last forever...

Until I heard Abe's heartbeat. It was fading. I pulled away from the Count and I looked at Abe on the floor.

"He's dying, isn't he?" I asked.

"Humans are dying from the moment of their birth," he said.

Abe groaned. I couldn't take my eyes off him until the Count took my chin and jerked my head back to him. He said, "But not you. Not anymore."

I never have to die, I thought.

He leaned down and licked the blood off my neck, and I

forgot Abe and everything else. It was just the Count and me again, alone in the world.

When he put my mouth against his throat, I bit him without even having to think about it. His blood gushed into my mouth, and it was warm, and it didn't taste like I imagined at all. It was the most wonderful taste in the world, like hot peppers and chocolate and bubbly champagne and life. I could not get enough of it.

I drank and I drank until the Count pulled me off, and I was so dizzy I collapsed on the floor.

I crawled over to Abe. I could hear his heartbeat again. I could feel how warm he was, even though he was far away.

When I touched him his heart sped up. I tasted his fear, and then I tasted his blood. It was different from the Count's, not as strong but still heavenly. Abe groaned, but he didn't try to stop me. I finished. I put Abe on my neck. He drank and I knew that he would be one of us. He wouldn't die. But the Count just laughed and said I wasn't strong enough to make a vampire and that Abe was too weak to make the transformation anyway.

I stared at Abe. His heart sounded stronger to me. Was the Count lying?

I felt hot and weak. The Count told me, "It is time for you to rest, Little One. Dawn has come and gone already, and I have much to do."

He pulled me to my feet and led me over to the coffin. He gave me a long kiss. It was wonderful like before. I had his blood in me now. The heat of it burned in me. I felt his heartbeat throbbing through my whole body. It was slow but much more powerful than mine or Abe's. My heart and the whole world slowed down to match the Count and still it was all one kiss and I melted into it and just let go...

But this time I knew it couldn't be good night. It had to be good-bye. Otherwise I was trapped. I would have to kill. Abe would wind up dead or he would be trapped, too. How could I trade the lives of all the people I would have to kill for my own immortality? This was probably the last moment I would ever be strong enough to know that.

I pulled the stake out of my pocket and buried it in the Count's chest. It slid in more easily than I expected now that I was so strong.

The Count staggered back and stared at me. He was surprised. I realized that was the first genuine expression I'd seen on his face. I don't think anything had surprised him that much in hundreds of years. I asked him if had predicted that, because humans in love are not as predictable as he thinks.

And he vanished, too, just like you did, one heartbeat at a time. As each heartbeat took him away from me I felt colder and sadder. I had killed him, and you, and my own chance of living forever.

Abe struggled over to my side, but I think he was afraid to

touch me. He wanted to know if we were vampires, but I reminded him of what Renfield said: "Kill the master and the fledglings are released."

I couldn't hear Abe's heartbeats anymore or even my own. I knew that we were released. I was human and mortal and cold and lonely. Abe took me in his arms and that helped, but it wasn't the same as the Count. And it won't ever be, will it?

We heard sirens then, and we bolted.

I picked up Mr. Bubbles on the way.

I'm going to take him to your tomb, the real one next to your mother, and put him in there.

I love you, Lucy. I always thought we'd go through every adventure together forever, that I would follow you into the darkest of places and back out again. But there are places too dark for me to stay.

I am so sorry for how everything ended up. I hope, wherever you are, that you are with your mother and at peace. I miss you.

Love always,
Mina.

From:	Mina Murray
To:	Jonathan Harker
Subject:	Good-bye
Sent:	June 27 11:59 PM

Jonathan,

We're done. The marks on my neck are healing. I bet yours are, too.

I wish you well. Be faithful to the next girl, Jonathan. It matters.

Mina

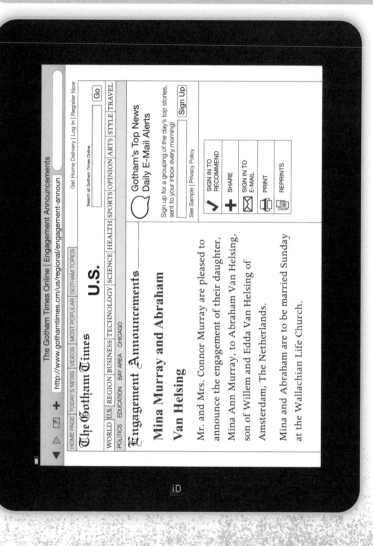

The Gotham Times Online | Engagement Announcements

http://www.gothamtimes.com/us/regional/engagement-announ

Get Home Delivery | Log In | Register Now

The Gotham Times

U.S.

Search all Gotham Times Online [Go]

HOME PAGE | TODAY'S NEWS | VIDEOS | MOST POPULAR | GOTHAM TOPICS

WORLD | U.S. | REGION | BUSINESS | TECHNOLOGY | SCIENCE | HEALTH | SPORTS | OPINION | ARTS | STYLE | TRAVEL
POLITICS   EDUCATION   BAY AREA   CHICAGO

Engagement Announcements

Mina Murray and Abraham Van Helsing

Mr. and Mrs. Connor Murray are pleased to announce the engagement of their daughter, Mina Ann Murray, to Abraham Van Helsing, son of Willem and Edda Van Helsing of Amsterdam, The Netherlands.

Mina and Abraham are to be married Sunday at the Wallachian Life Church.

Gotham's Top News
Daily E-Mail Alerts

Sign up for a grouping of the day's top stories, sent to your inbox every morning!

[Sign Up]

See Sample | Privacy Policy

✓ SIGN IN TO RECOMMEND

+ SHARE

✉ SIGN IN TO E-MAIL

🖨 PRINT

▤ REPRINTS

iD

ABOUT THE AUTHOR

After a childhood often spent without electricity or running water, Bekka Black escaped the beautiful wilderness of Talkeetna, Alaska, for indoor plumbing and 24/7 electricity in Berlin, Germany. Accustomed to the cushy lifestyle, she discovered the Internet in college and has been wasting time on it ever since (when not frittering away her time on her iPhone). Somehow, she manages to write novels, including the award-winning Hannah Vogel mystery series set, in all places, 1930s Berlin. The series has received numerous starred reviews and the first book, *A Trace of Smoke*, was chosen as a *Writer's Digest* Notable Debut. She lives in Hawaii with her husband, son, two cats, and too many geckos to count. *iDrakula* is her first cell phone novel.